RICKY RICOTTA'S

MIGHTY ROBOT

vs. THE URANIUM UNICORNS FROM URANUS

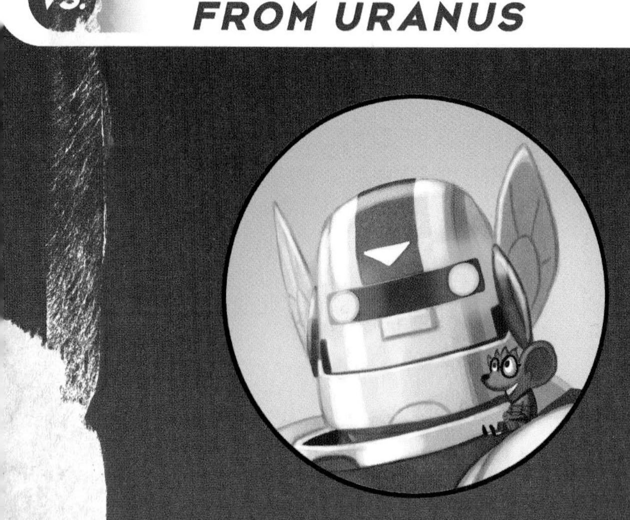

STORY BY

DAV PILKEY

ART BY

DAN SANTAT

FOR QUAID, WILL, AND DANNY O'BRIEN
– D.P.

FOR ALL THE TEACHERS AND
LIBRARIANS OUT THERE WHO CONTINUE
TO FIGHT THE GOOD FIGHT
– D.S.

Library of Congress Cataloging-in-Publication Data

Pilkey, Dav, 1966 – author.
Ricky Ricotta's mighty robot vs. the uranium unicorns from Uranus /
story by Dav Pilkey ; art by Dan Santat. — Revised edition.
pages cm
Summary: Evil Uncle Unicorn attempts to dominate earth by using a Ladybot to trick Mighty Robot.
ISBN 978-0-545-63015-3
1. Ricotta, Ricky (Fictitious character) — Juvenile fiction. 2. Mice — Juvenile fiction.
3. Robots — Juvenile fiction. 4. Heroes — Juvenile fiction. 5. Friendship — Juvenile fiction.
6. Unicorns — Juvenile fiction. 7. Uranus (Planet) — Juvenile fiction. [1. Mice — Fiction.
2. Robots — Fiction. 3. Heroes — Fiction. 4. Humorous stories.] I. Santat, Dan, illustrator.
II. Title. III. Title: Ricky Ricotta's mighty robot versus the uranium unicorns from Uranus.
PZ7.P63123Rtt 2014 813.54 — dc23 2014003716

10 9 8 7 6 5 4 3 2 1 15 16 17 18 19/0

Printed in the U.S.A. 40

Revised edition
First printing, July 2015

Book design by Phil Falco

CHAPTERS

CHAPTER ONE
FUN . . . AND NOT FUN

One sunny morning, a little mouse named Ricky Ricotta went out to play with his giant Mighty Robot.

First, they came to the playground.

The Mighty Robot pushed Ricky on the swing set.

"This is fun," said Ricky.

Then Ricky tried to push his Robot on the swing set.

"This is not fun," said Ricky.

Next, Ricky and his Robot flew to the amusement park.

Ricky got on the Ferris wheel.

"This is fun!" said Ricky.

Then Ricky's Mighty Robot got on the Ferris wheel.

"This is not fun," said Ricky.

Finally, Ricky and his Mighty
Robot went to the swimming pool.
Ricky did a perfect swan dive.
"That was fun!" said Ricky.

Then Ricky's Robot jumped in, too.

All of the water splashed out of the pool.

“That was *NOT FUN*,” said Ricky.

CHAPTER TWO
THE WISH

Ricky and his Mighty Robot walked home. Ricky was not happy.

That night after supper, Ricky's Mighty Robot helped Ricky get ready for bed.

Usually Ricky enjoyed brushing
his teeth with the Turbo-Toothbrush
built into his Robot's index finger . . .

. . . but not tonight.

Usually Ricky laughed when his Robot helped him put on his pajamas . . .

. . . but not tonight.

And usually Ricky had fun when his Robot tucked him into bed . . .

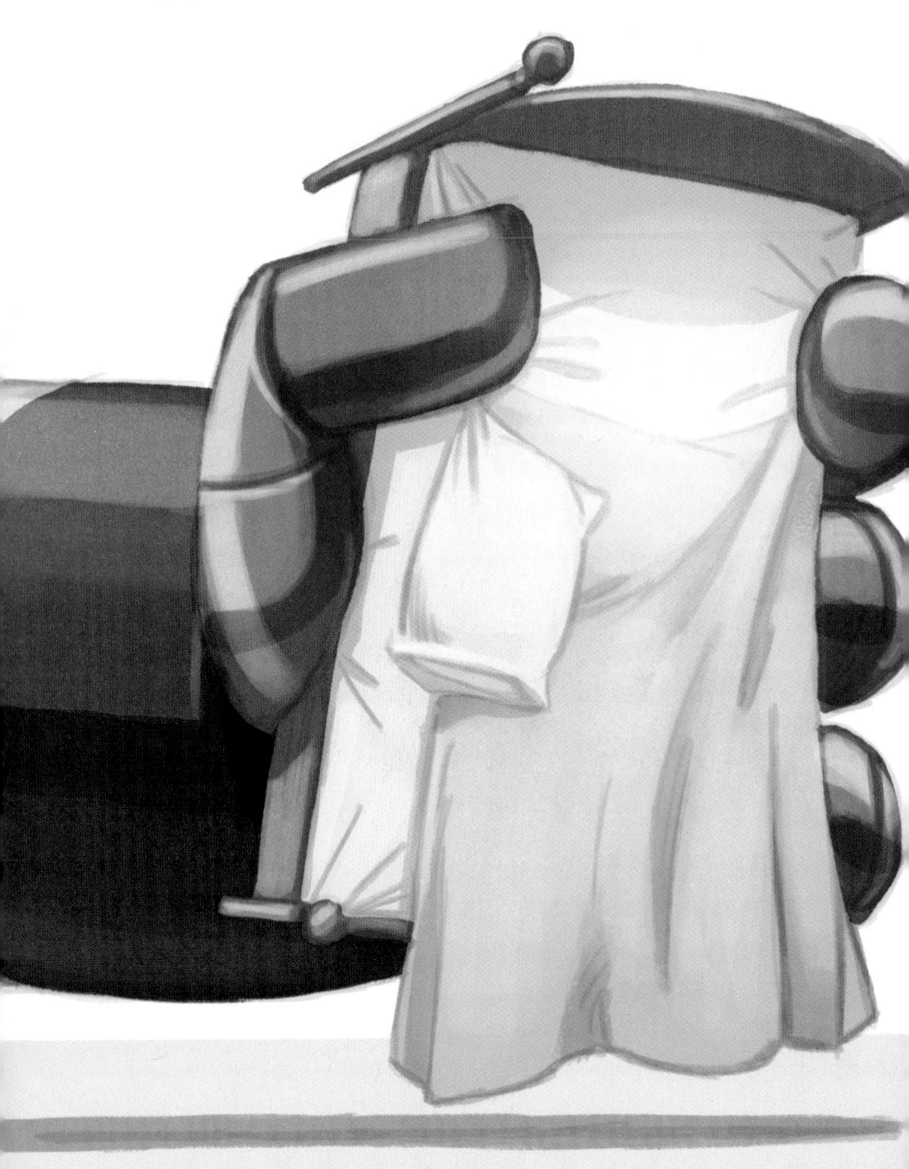

. . . but not tonight.

Ricky loved his Mighty Robot, but sometimes it was hard having a best friend who was so *BIG*.

“I wish my Mighty Robot had somebody his own size to play with,” Ricky whispered. “Then maybe I could have fun by myself.”

As Ricky went to sleep that evening, he did not suspect that his wish was about to come true.

CHAPTER THREE
UNCLE UNICORN

At that very moment, about 1,650 million miles away on a planet called Uranus, a nasty creature named Uncle Unicorn was hatching a hideous plan.

Uncle Unicorn was the president of Unicorp Inc. He had made a lot of money by turning his planet into a nuclear dumping ground.

All over the galaxy, creatures came to unload their toxic waste onto Uranus.

Most of the Unicorns who lived on Uranus had moved away a long time ago. But the three who remained had mutated into gigantic Uranium Unicorns, and they served their evil boss with glee.

That night, Uncle Unicorn looked out at his planet through the window of his tall office building. “I’ve destroyed my entire planet,” he laughed. “Now I shall take over the Earth.”

Uncle Unicorn knew about Ricky's Mighty Robot. He knew that the evilest minds in the galaxy had tried to fight Ricky's Robot and failed.

"But I've got a trick that's SURE to stop Ricky Ricotta's Mighty Robot once and for all!" snarled Uncle Unicorn.

Uncle Unicorn took his three Uranium Unicorns into his rocket ship and blasted off toward Earth.

CHAPTER FOUR
THE LADYBOT

The next day, Ricky ran outside to wake up his Mighty Robot.

"Mighty Robot!" cried Ricky. "You got a present! You got a present!"

Ricky's Robot threw off his pajamas and ran to see the giant present.

"I wonder who it is from," said Ricky.

Ricky's Mighty Robot opened up the present.

Inside was a giant Ladybot.

She was big and pink, and she had a giant heart on her chest.

Suddenly, the heart began to glow and a laser beam shot out. It zapped Ricky's Robot right in his eyes.

"Hey!" shouted Ricky. "What's the big idea?"

The giant heart stopped glowing, and the Ladybot returned to normal. But Ricky's Mighty Robot was not normal anymore. He had changed. He had a funny look in his eyes. He was *in LOVE*!

The Ladybot held out her hand, and Ricky's Mighty Robot took it. Then, together, the two Robots turned and skipped away down the street.

BOOM! BOOM! BOOM!

"Mighty Robot!" called Ricky. "Come back here!"

But Ricky's Mighty Robot was gone.

CHAPTER FIVE
ALONE

Ricky tried to follow his Mighty Robot, but he could not keep up.

"Hey, wait for me!" Ricky called.

But the two Robots did not wait.

Ricky was all alone.

That night, Ricky's Mighty Robot did not come home for supper.

He was not there to help Ricky brush his teeth . . .

. . . or put on his pajamas . . .

. . . or tuck him into bed.

"Would you like us to tuck you in tonight?" asked Ricky's parents.

"No, thank you," said Ricky.

And he went to sleep with a sad heart.

CHAPTER SIX
THE NEXT DAY

The next day, Ricky went looking for his Mighty Robot. He searched all over town, but he could not find his Robot anywhere.

Then Ricky hiked into the woods.

Deep inside the forest, Ricky finally found his Mighty Robot.

But as he got closer, Ricky discovered something horrible. His Mighty Robot had been captured.

"A-*HA*!" said Ricky. "I *KNEW* that Ladybot was up to no good!"

Suddenly, the Ladybot's giant heart opened up, and Uncle Unicorn peeked out.

"Now that we've got that Mighty Robot under the spell of our evil Hypno-Ray," said Uncle Unicorn, "he won't be able to stop our terrible plans! But just to be on the safe side, I want you Uranium Unicorns to DESTROY him!"

"OH, NO!" gasped Ricky. "I've got to save my Mighty Robot!"

CHAPTER SEVEN
HELP IS ON THE WAY

Ricky ran back through the woods and all the way to the other side of town. Finally, he reached his cousin Lucy's house.

Lucy was in the backyard playing with her pet Jurassic Jackrabbits, Fudgie, Cupcake, and Waffles.

"Hi, Ricky," said Lucy. "Do you want to play *princess?*"

"*NO!*" cried Ricky, panting hard and out of breath. "I . . . NEED . . . TO . . . BORROW . . . WAFFLES!"

"Come on, Waffles," said Lucy. "This looks like an emergency!"

Lucy and Ricky climbed onto Waffles's back and prepared for takeoff.

Fudgie and Cupcake wanted to help, too, but Lucy told them to stay home.

AW, YOU GUYS FEEL LEFT OUT, DON'TCHA?

HMMM...

I'VE GOT IT!

YOU TWO HAVE A VERY IMPORTANT JOB TODAY!

I NEED YOU TO STAY HERE AND GUARD THESE COOKIES!

...AND WHATEVER YOU DO...

DON'T EAT 'EM!

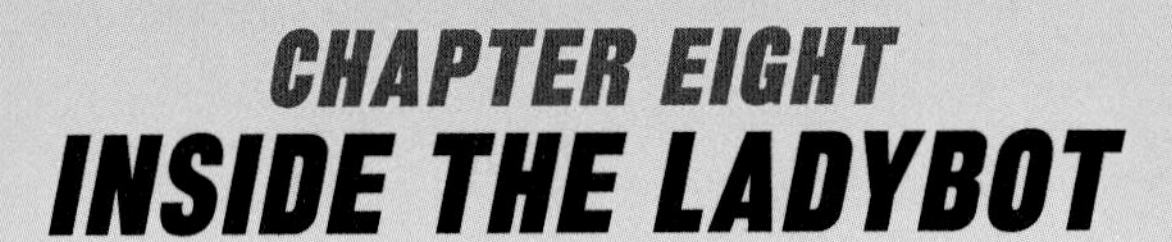

CHAPTER EIGHT
INSIDE THE LADYBOT

Soon, Ricky, Lucy, and Waffles reached the woods. There they saw Ricky's Mighty Robot being held by the Uranium Unicorns.

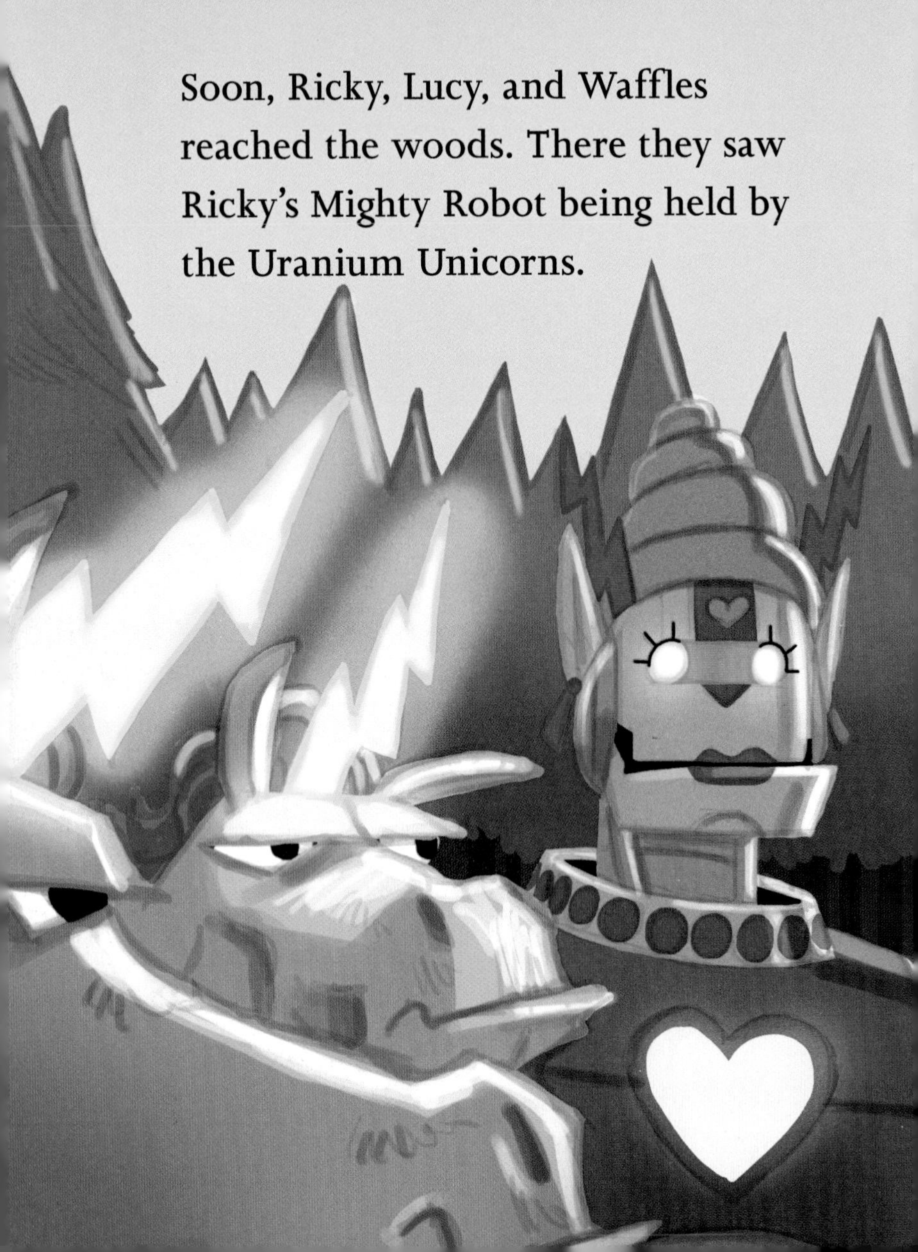

"My Mighty Robot has been hypnotized," said Ricky. "And those evil Unicorn guys are going to destroy him!"

"But what can we do?" asked Lucy.

"We've got to stop that giant Ladybot now!" said Ricky. "She's controlling my Robot with a Hypno-Ray!"

Waffles landed carefully on the Ladybot's shoulder.

Ricky and Lucy climbed into the Ladybot's cheek and looked around for a way to turn off the Hypno-Ray.

Suddenly, Uncle Unicorn found Ricky and Lucy.

"So, you thought you could save the day, huh?" laughed Uncle Unicorn. "Well, you were WRONG!" Uncle Unicorn tied up Ricky and Lucy and hung them high above the main generator.

Ricky looked down. “If only there were some way I could destroy that generator,” said Ricky. “But how?”

CHAPTER NINE
THE GENERATOR

Just then, a few drops of sweat dripped from Ricky's face. They fell down into the generator. Suddenly, a giant spark flashed out of the generator, followed by a puff of black smoke. The generator stopped for a split second, then continued running.

"A-*HA*!" cried Ricky. "If I can get that generator wet, it will shut down!"

Ricky tried to sweat more, but he couldn't. He tried to spit into the generator, but his mouth was too dry.

"Lucy," said Ricky, "you've got to spit down onto that generator!"

"No way!" said Lucy. "Princesses do *NOT* spit!"

"*Pleeeeease?*" Ricky begged. "It's a matter of life and death!" But Lucy still refused.

Then, Ricky got a sneaky idea.

"Just think," said Ricky. "If those Unicorns destroy the planet, there will be no more ice cream and no more chocolate chip cookies . . ."

"N-n-no more ice cream?" Lucy whimpered. Her eyes welled up with tears. "N-n-no more chocolate chip cookies?"

Giant teardrops began dripping down Lucy's face.

"And no more cotton candy and coconut cream pie," said Ricky. "And no more vanilla wafers and grape lollipops."

"N-n-no m-m-more g-g-grape lollipops?" cried Lucy.

Suddenly, Lucy burst into tears. Giant tears sprayed from her face and fell down into the generator below.

Bright sparks and horrible black smoke began shooting out of the generator. It shook back and forth. Then, finally, it broke down.

"Hooray!" shouted Ricky.

CHAPTER TEN
RICKY'S ROBOT RETURNS

The generator was broken, the Ladybot had shut down, and the Hypno-Ray had stopped working. Suddenly, Ricky's Mighty Robot returned to normal.

The Mighty Robot did not know where he was, or what was going on, but he knew he had to save the day.

With a mighty burst of Robo-Power, Ricky's Robot snapped his chains. Then, they all started to fight.

The big, bad beasties banded together and blasted the Robot's behind.

So Ricky's Robot unleashed an
ultra-unbeatable Unicorn uppercut.

Then the plucky protector prevailed by punching the putrid ponies into a perilous pile-up.

The Uranium Unicorns were very angry.

"No more horsing around," they said. "It's time to kick some Robot tushy!"

CHAPTER ELEVEN
THE BIG BATTLE
(IN FLIP-O-RAMA™)

FLIP-O

HEY, KIDS! YOU CAN ANIMATE THE ACTION BY FOLLOWING THESE EASY STEPS!

-RAMA

HERE'S HOW IT WORKS!

STEP 1

Place your *left* hand inside the dotted lines marked "LEFT HAND HERE." Hold the book open *flat*.

STEP 2

Grasp the *right-hand* page with your right thumb and index finger (inside the dotted lines marked "RIGHT THUMB HERE").

STEP 3

Now *quickly* flip the right-hand page back and forth until the picture appears to be *animated*.

(For extra fun, try adding your own sound-effects!)

FLIP-O-RAMA 1

(pages 77 and 79)

Remember, flip *only* page 77.
While you are flipping, be sure you
can see the picture on page 77
and the one on page 79.
If you flip quickly, the two
pictures will start to look like
one *animated* picture.

Don't forget to add
your own sound-effects!

LEFT HAND HERE

THE URANIUM UNICORNS ATTACKED.

RIGHT THUMB HERE

RIGHT
INDEX
FINGER
HERE

THE URANIUM UNICORNS ATTACKED.

FLIP-O-RAMA 2

(pages 81 and 83)

Remember, flip *only* page 81.
While you are flipping, be sure you
can see the picture on page 81
and the one on page 83.
If you flip quickly, the two
pictures will start to look like
one *animated* picture.

Don't forget to add
your own sound-effects!

LEFT HAND HERE

RICKY'S MIGHTY ROBOT FOUGHT BACK.

RIGHT THUMB HERE

RIGHT
INDEX
FINGER
HERE

RICKY'S MIGHTY ROBOT FOUGHT BACK.

FLIP-O-RAMA 3

(pages 85 and 87)

Remember, flip *only* page 85.
While you are flipping, be sure you
can see the picture on page 85
and the one on page 87.
If you flip quickly, the two
pictures will start to look like
one *animated* picture.

Don't forget to add
your own sound-effects!

LEFT HAND HERE

THE URANIUM UNICORNS BATTLED HARD.

RIGHT THUMB HERE

RIGHT
INDEX
FINGER
HERE

THE URANIUM UNICORNS BATTLED HARD.

FLIP-O-RAMA 4

(pages 89 and 91)

Remember, flip *only* page 89.
While you are flipping, be sure you
can see the picture on page 89
and the one on page 91.
If you flip quickly, the two
pictures will start to look like
one *animated* picture.

Don't forget to add
your own sound-effects!

LEFT HAND HERE

RICKY'S MIGHTY ROBOT BATTLED HARDER.

RIGHT THUMB HERE

RIGHT
INDEX
FINGER
HERE

RICKY'S MIGHTY ROBOT BATTLED HARDER.

FLIP-O-RAMA 5

(pages 93 and 95)

Remember, flip *only* page 93.
While you are flipping, be sure you
can see the picture on page 93
and the one on page 95.
If you flip quickly, the two
pictures will start to look like
one *animated* picture.

Don't forget to add
your own sound-effects!

LEFT HAND HERE

RICKY'S MIGHTY ROBOT WON THE WAR.

RIGHT THUMB HERE

RIGHT
INDEX
FINGER
HERE

RICKY'S MIGHTY ROBOT WON THE WAR.

CHAPTER TWELVE
THE SUPER MECHA-EVIL LADYBOT

Ricky's Mighty Robot had defeated the Uranium Unicorns, but Uncle Unicorn was not ready to give up just yet.

Quickly, he turned on the backup generator, and then he pressed a secret button on his control panel.

CH-KLICK
WRRRRRRR

VZZZZZ
VZZZZZ
SHOOOOM

K-KUNG
K-KUNG
FSSSSSS
FSSSSSS

WRRRRR

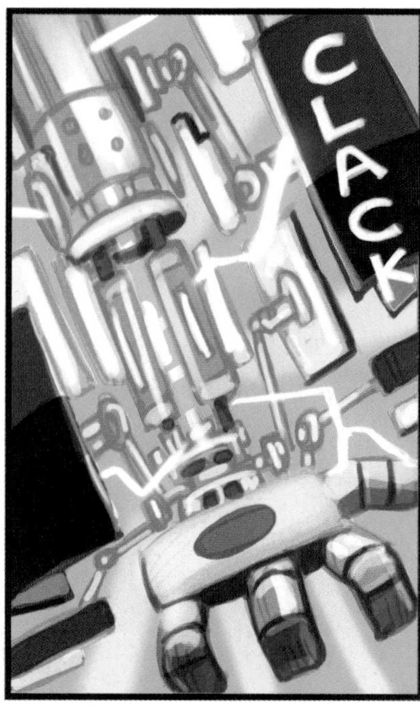
CLACK

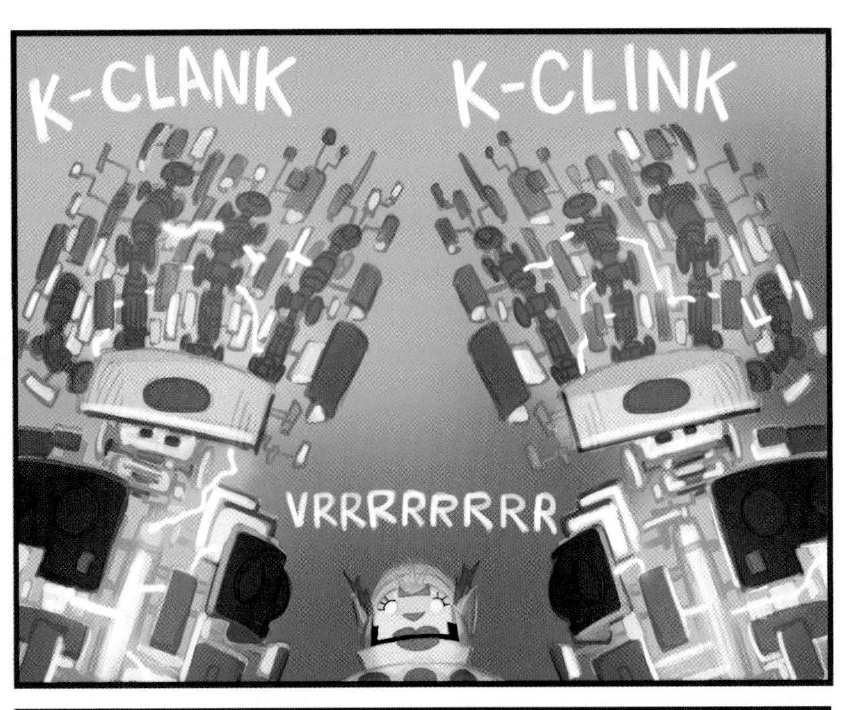
K-CLANK
K-CLINK
VRRRRRRR

K-KONG

WHOOOOSH

K-BLONG

RUMBLE
RUMBLE

REMEMBER---
GUARD THE COOKIES
BUT DON'T EAT 'EM!

DON'T EAT 'EM!
DON'T EAT 'EM!
DON'T EAT 'EM!
DON'T EAT 'EM!

MULMP
UMMP

THUMPA
THUMPA
THUMPA
THUMPA THUMPA
THUMPA

THUMPA
THUMPA
THUMPA

THUMPA
THUMPA
THUMPA
THUMPA

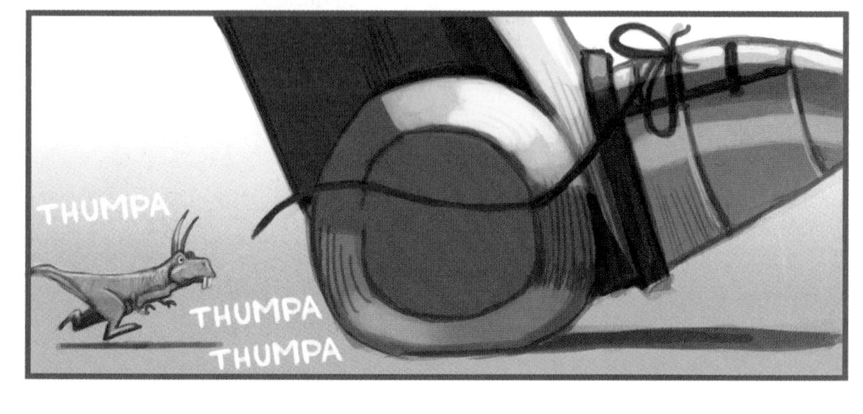
THUMPA
THUMPA
THUMPA

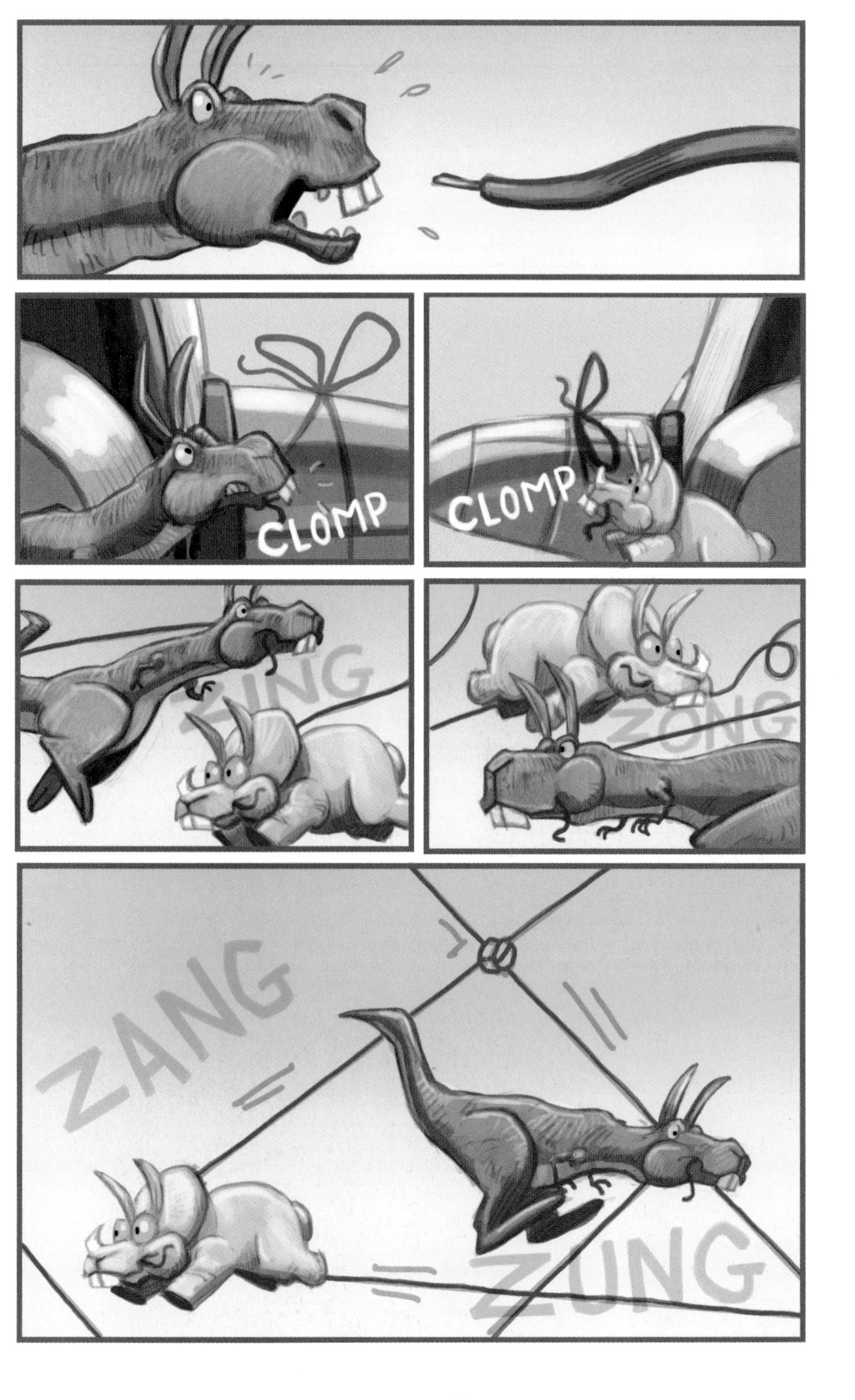
CLOMP
CLOMP
ZING
ZONG
ZANG
ZUNG

FINALLY, THE MIGHTY ROBOT REACHED A STEEP MOUNTAIN.

THERE WAS NO PLACE LEFT TO RUN.

THE LADYBOT TRIED TO LIFT HER MASSIVE FOOT...

...AND CAME CRASHING TO THE GROUND.

Ricky and Lucy untied their ropes and ran out of the Ladybot's cheek.

Uncle Unicorn chased after them . . .

. . . but Ricky's Mighty Robot stopped him just in time.

"My beautiful Ladybot is destroyed!" cried Uncle Unicorn. "How did it happen?"

"It looks like somebody tied her shoelaces together," said Ricky.

"But who could have done that?" asked Lucy.

Just then, Fudgie and Cupcake poked their heads out of the bushes. They had been helpful after all.

"Hooray for Fudgie and Cupcake!" cried Lucy.

WELL, BOYS, IT LOOKS LIKE YOU SAVED THE DAY!

BUT DID YOU SAVE THOSE COOKIES?

YOU DIDN'T EAT THEM, DID YOU?

WELL??

WHERE ARE THEY THEN?

BLEEEAH

EWW...
YOU GUYS ARE DISGUSTING!

CHAPTER THIRTEEN
JUSTICE PREVAILS

Ricky's Mighty Robot stuffed the three Uranium Unicorns into their rocket ship and threw it back to Uranus.

Then he picked up the giant Ladybot and threw her back, too.

Finally, they all took Uncle Unicorn to the Squeakyville jail, which was getting very crowded.

Ricky and his Mighty Robot flew Lucy and her Jurassic Jackrabbits back to their house.

"Do you want to stay and play *princess?*" asked Lucy.

"No, thanks," said Ricky. "I've got something important to do!"

And, together, the two friends flew home.

CHAPTER FOURTEEN
BEDTIME

That night after supper, Ricky helped his Mighty Robot get ready for bed.

Ricky brushed his Mighty Robot's giant teeth . . .

. . . then he helped his Mighty Robot put on his pajamas . . .

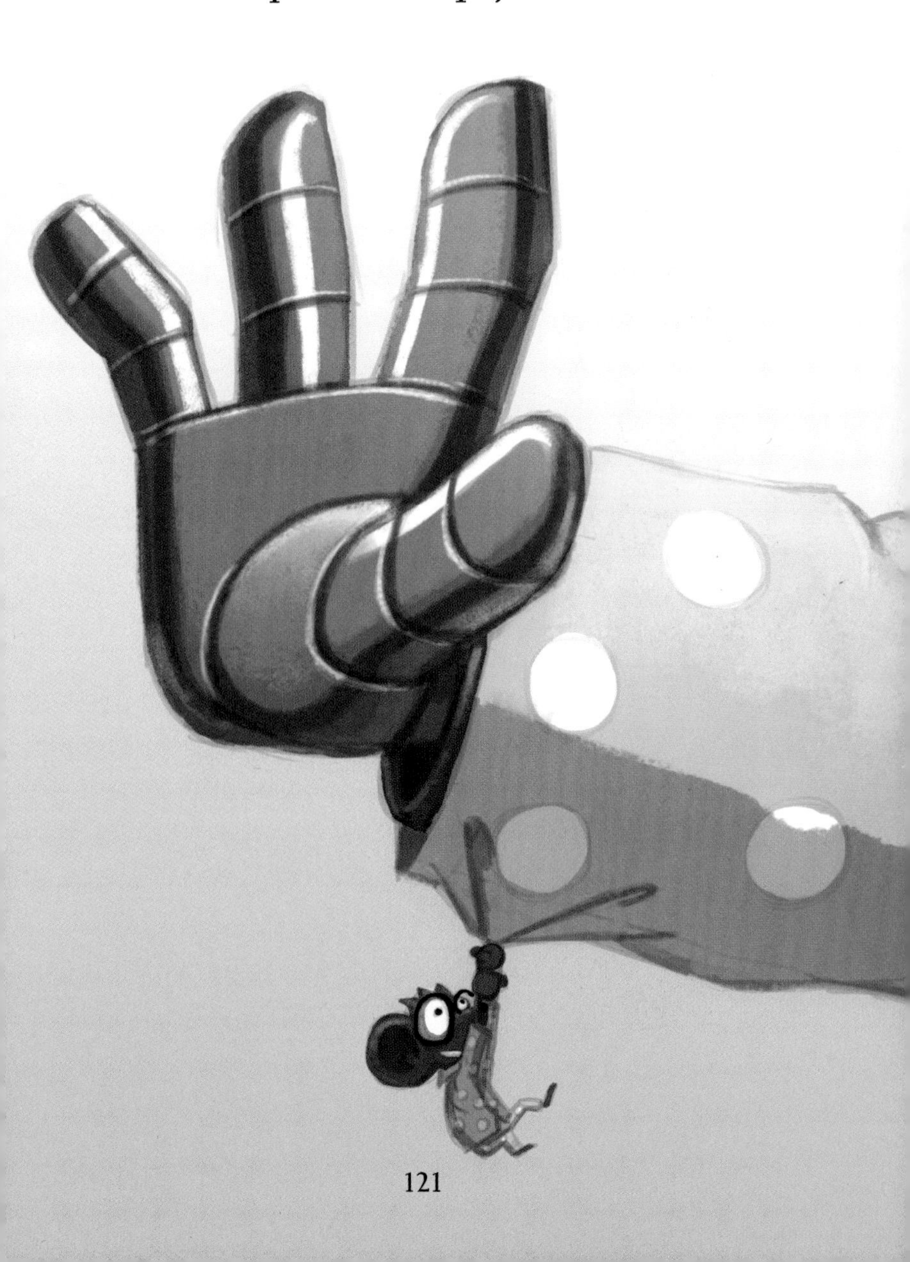

. . . and, finally, he tucked his
Mighty Robot into bed.

“I’m glad you boys are having fun again,” said Ricky’s father, “even though you are both very different.”

“Me, too,” said Ricky . . .

. . . "that's what friends are for."

READY FOR

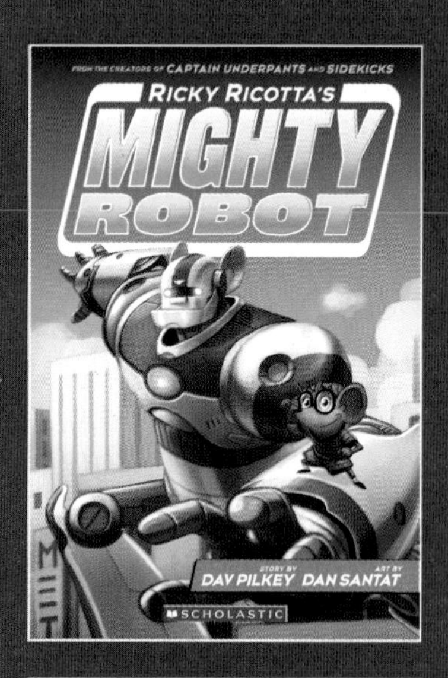
FROM THE CREATORS OF CAPTAIN UNDERPANTS AND SIDEKICKS
RICKY RICOTTA'S
MIGHTY ROBOT
STORY BY DAV PILKEY
ART BY DAN SANTAT
SCHOLASTIC

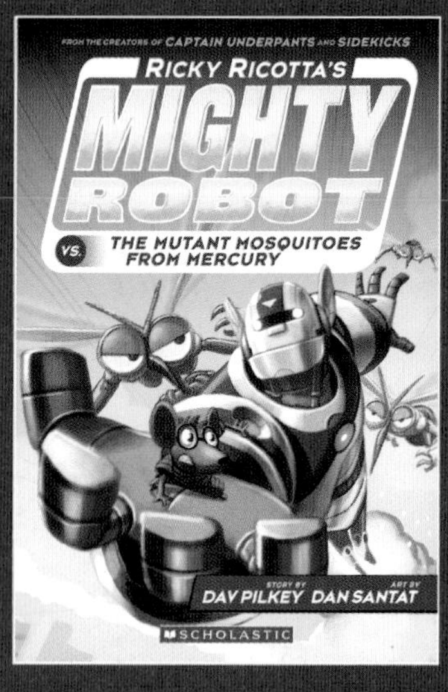
FROM THE CREATORS OF CAPTAIN UNDERPANTS AND SIDEKICKS
RICKY RICOTTA'S
MIGHTY ROBOT
VS. THE MUTANT MOSQUITOES FROM MERCURY
STORY BY DAV PILKEY
ART BY DAN SANTAT
SCHOLASTIC

FROM THE CREATORS OF CAPTAIN UNDERPANTS AND SIDEKICKS
RICKY RICOTTA'S
MIGHTY ROBOT
VS. THE VOODOO VULTURES FROM VENUS
STORY BY DAV PILKEY
ART BY DAN SANTAT
SCHOLASTIC

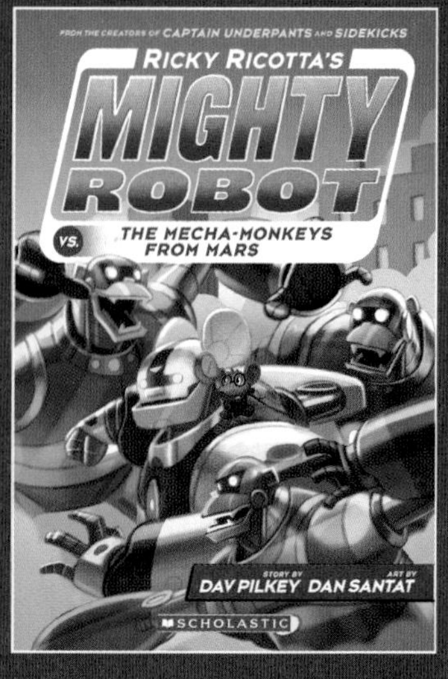
FROM THE CREATORS OF CAPTAIN UNDERPANTS AND SIDEKICKS
RICKY RICOTTA'S
MIGHTY ROBOT
VS. THE MECHA-MONKEYS FROM MARS
STORY BY DAV PILKEY
ART BY DAN SANTAT
SCHOLASTIC

MORE RICKY?

FROM THE CREATORS OF CAPTAIN UNDERPANTS AND SIDEKICKS
RICKY RICOTTA'S
MIGHTY ROBOT
VS. THE JURASSIC JACKRABBITS FROM JUPITER
STORY BY DAV PILKEY
ART BY DAN SANTAT
SCHOLASTIC

FROM THE CREATORS OF CAPTAIN UNDERPANTS AND SIDEKICKS
RICKY RICOTTA'S
MIGHTY ROBOT
VS. THE STUPID STINKBUGS FROM SATURN
STORY BY DAV PILKEY
ART BY DAN SANTAT
SCHOLASTIC

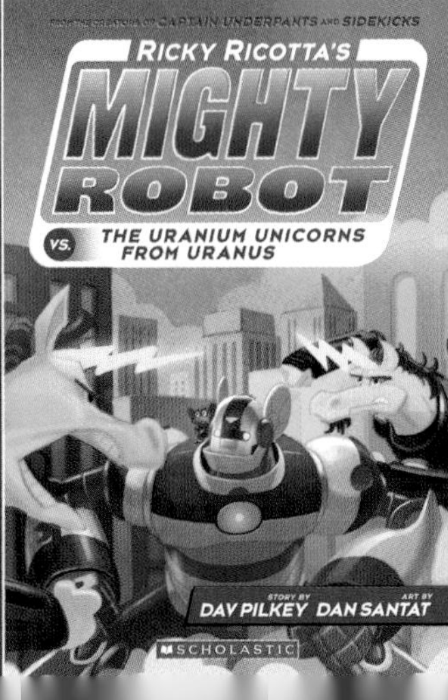
CAPTAIN UNDERPANTS AND SIDEKICKS
RICKY RICOTTA'S
MIGHTY ROBOT
VS. THE URANIUM UNICORNS FROM URANUS
STORY BY DAV PILKEY
ART BY DAN SANTAT
SCHOLASTIC

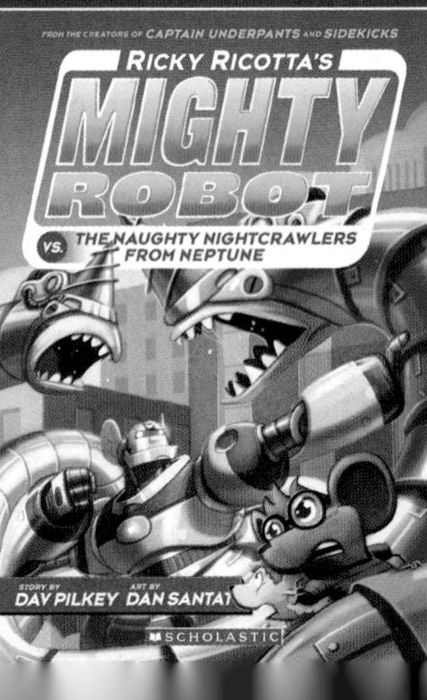
FROM THE CREATORS OF CAPTAIN UNDERPANTS AND SIDEKICKS
RICKY RICOTTA'S
MIGHTY ROBOT
VS. THE NAUGHTY NIGHTCRAWLERS FROM NEPTUNE
STORY BY DAV PILKEY
ART BY DAN SANTAT
SCHOLASTIC

DAV PILKEY

has written and illustrated more than fifty books for children, including *The Paperboy*, a Caldecott Honor book; *Dog Breath: The Horrible Trouble with Hally Tosis*, winner of the California Young Reader Medal; and the IRA Children's Choice Dumb Bunnies series. He is also the creator of the *New York Times* bestselling Captain Underpants books. Dav lives in the Pacific Northwest with his wife. Find him online at www.pilkey.com.

DAN SANTAT

is the writer and illustrator of the *New York Times* bestselling picture book *The Adventures of Beekle: The Unimaginary Friend*, which was awarded the Caldecott Medal. He is also the creator of the graphic novel *Sidekicks* and has illustrated many acclaimed picture books, including *Because I'm Your Dad* by Ahmet Zappa and *Crankenstein* by Samantha Berger. Dan also created the Disney animated hit *The Replacements*. He lives in Southern California with his family. Find him online at www.dantat.com.

HAVING A REALLY
BIG BEST FRIEND
ISN'T ALWAYS BIG FUN . . .

Ricky Ricotta loves his Mighty Robot, but sometimes it's hard to have such a big buddy! If only the Mighty Robot could find someone his own size to play with, Ricky might finally have some fun by himself. Little does Ricky know, his wish is about to come true. Evil Uncle Unicorn is hatching a hideous plan to take over Earth, and he's got a supersized surprise for Ricky and his Robot!

FEATURING FLIP-O-RAMA!
FLIP THE PAGES TO ANIMATE THE ACTION!
PLUS: ALL-NEW MINI COMICS INSIDE!

PRAISE FOR
RICKY RICOTTA'S MIGHTY ROBOT

"A fun introduction to chapter books."
– *School Library Journal*

"Has all the classic Pilkey hallmarks: comic book panels, superhero action, and Flip-O-Rama."
– *Booklist*

£4.99
ISBN 978-1-4071-4339-2
00499
EAN
9 781407 143392

SCHOLASTIC
www.scholastic.com/rickyricotta

Cover design by Phil Falco